The Disciple

The Hand of God, Volume 1

Darin S. Cape

Published by SHP Comics, 2023.

THE DISCIPLE

First edition. November 1, 2023.

ISBN: 979-8223608400

Written by Darin S. Cape.

The Disciple

How can we discover the ultimate source of life in the universe? Each revelation unfolds exponentially more dimensions of possibility. It is not within our capacity, as human beings, to advance any set of facts with either epistemological or teleological certainty. Happily, we must be content with the endless quest for knowledge.

– Dr. Samuel J. Friedmann

Director of Xenobiology International Marine Exploration Institute

• • • •

EVERY NIGHT, BEFORE I fell asleep, Jesus appeared at the foot of my bed. His long hair touched his shoulders, his eyes were kind and bright, and he wore a rough, gray robe that faded to white around the edges. He was exactly like Mama's pictures of him. The first night he visited, I asked if he could see my Daddy on Mars. He said yes. When I asked what Mars was like, he said it was dry and rocky—like Nazareth.

When I told Mama, she said it was a sin to make up stories about Jesus. But Jesus still came to visit me every night. He said Daddy was good, but he missed me. When Mama asked if Jesus came to visit me again, I lied and said no. Maybe she knew I was lying, because the next night she put a snake in my room.

In the morning, I saw the snake curled up in the blanket at my feet. I'd seen lots of snakes before and I knew it was a copperhead. I wasn't afraid. They won't hurt you unless you bother them. Its eyes stared at me from beneath the covers. It was Mama's way of testing me to see if I was telling the truth about Jesus.

• • • •

A DECADE LATER, JOHN Haggerty stood on the edge of his mother's grave, his fingers slowly released a handful of dirt. All the faithful, her only friends, were in attendance. Waves of conflicting emotions rushed through John as her coffin was lowered into the earth, but mostly, he felt relief. She was gone, and with her, the guilt he had carried with him since he was a child. He couldn't remember a time when he didn't feel guilty, guilty for not being devout enough, pure enough, or selfless enough to satisfy her. He resented living in a rundown shack that leaked in the summer and was drafty in the winter. He hated being hungry and poor and he hated her for driving his father away.

Colton Dixon, known locally as the Old Blind Pig, stood next to him, a snake wrapped between his fingers as he muttered in tongues. John remembered the first time he saw Colton handle a snake. He watched with fascination and terror as the serpent slithered between Colton's fingers, its forked tongue flashing out and disappearing again. Now, as a student of biology, he just felt sorry for the snake. Looking around at the congregation, he was overwhelmed by pity and disgust. A few more hours and he would be on a plane back to Boston and could, finally, leave his childhood behind.

John's mother was passionately devoted to God, but God hadn't put food on the table, nor did prayer keep her from getting sick as her body wasted away. John only visited her once during the two years of her prolonged illness. He found her lying on dirty bed sheets, her body decimated, the smell of urine filling the room. Church members delivered meals once a day, washed her body, and prayed with her. When he arrived, John barely recognized her gaunt form, except for her eyes, which still shone with the light of a true believer. Her suffering was further proof of her devotion. It made him sick.

The first day, he cleaned everything in the house, as if he could wash away all her pain and suffering. The smell of bleach filled the house, stinging his nose, and he wished there was something else that he could do. For two weeks, John shuffled around the small room as his mother read from the Bible and prayed. He knew she wanted him to join her, but he couldn't, that was something he could never do. Never again would he supplicate himself to a heartless God. He only asked her once to go to a hospital, knowing it would be in vain. He wanted to cry, to throw his arms around her, to beg her to seek treatment. "Please, mama." There were so many things he wanted to say but couldn't.

Finally, mercifully, she died. He sat holding her hands, looking into her eyes as she gasped slowly, her mouth opening and closing in vain, like a fish on land struggling to draw in a quickening breath. She drew one final gasp, looked at him, and fell back on the bed, the light in her eyes extinguished. He sat next to her for a long time and wept. He cried for himself, for the passing of this woman he hated and loved. He cried for her wasted life, for her devotion to a pitiless God. Why had He made her suffer, this poor pathetic woman. Was she now reaping her reward in Heaven? He wanted to believe it was possible.

John, now nineteen years old, was alone in the world. His father had died ten years earlier in an explosion caused by a gas leak at the icehouse prototype facility he was constructing on Mars. John saw the letter marked "International Space Exploration Agency," and knowing it was about his father, he secretly steamed it open. He read the formal announcement describing his father's death, then resealed it for his mother to find when she returned home. That evening, she burned the letter without opening it or saying a word.

John's relationship with Jesus ended when he was twelve. His mind rebelled against his mother's strict control. He spent more time away from home, taking long walks in the woods when he wasn't in school. He often saw Colton during his rambles, sitting by himself, listening to the forest. Colton could sit for hours in the same position. John would pass him on his way out in the morning and find him in the same position that afternoon when he returned for lunch.

One day, John asked Colton to join him on his walk. Colton nodded and followed him without saying a word. While Colton never spoke that day, John found his company soothing, and soon they walked together almost every day. Blind since birth, Colton possessed an extraordinary ability to perceive any critter they passed in the woods. As they walked the rambling paths, Colton would tap John quietly on the shoulder and point. Following Colton's finger with his eyes, John would be rewarded with a brief glimpse of one of the many denizens of the forest: a mink sliding into the river, a toad poking its head out of a hole, a snake slithering through the fallen leaves, or a bird alighting from a branch.

Colton taught John to be patient and observant. After walking for a while, they would find a spot to rest and sit quietly. Initially, John couldn't stay still for more than a few minutes, but as soon as he began to fidget, Colton would place his large hand on his shoulder. Colton's touch was calming, as if his hand could drain away John's nervous energy, tethering him to the moment. John's conscious mind would recede into the background, and he became aware of the patterns and activity around him: water running, a breeze rustling through the trees, birds singing, insects feeding, and predators of all sizes patiently stalking their prey.

Spending time with Colton in the woods was as close as John would come to a religious experience. In these moments, he felt the divinity of creation and could see himself as he truly was—a single life among the billions of creatures that inhabited the Earth. John found comfort in this feeling of insignificance. It freed him from the constant obligation to do God's will, as well as the guilt of never being able to live up to God's expectations. His mother's God was wrathful and vindictive, eager to punish every transgression. Her concept of God made John feel weak, helpless, and sinful. Being with Colton made John feel calm and connected to the Earth and its inhabitants.

After several months, Colton began to teach John how to handle serpents. Whenever they encountered a snake, Colton would get close to the ground and reach out his hand. At first, John thought the snake would strike, but Colton's movements were slow and unthreatening as he allowed the snake to explore his hand and arm with its tongue. The serpent would gradually curl itself around Colton's arm, resting its head in the crook of his elbow. When John was ready, he held out his hand, allowing the snake to explore his fingers. Usually, the snake would remain on Colton's arm, but occasionally, it would slide its head between John's fingers and slowly make its way up his forearm.

A few months after John handled his first snake in the woods, Colton gave him one to handle during church. His mother beamed as she watched her son carry the snake down the aisle. He had finally found his calling. That night, she read to him from Mark 16, "These signs will accompany those who have believed: in My name they will cast out demons, they will speak with new tongues; they will pick up serpents, and if they drink any deadly poison, it will not hurt them; they will lay hands on the sick, and they will recover." Most importantly, she no longer questioned him about his long absences from the house. He was doing the Lord's work now.

By age fifteen, John had learned how to act like a devoted servant of God and an obedient son, yet a deep chasm grew between him and his mother. He was receiving more respect within the church but was losing his faith. His mother didn't understand the transformation within him or how he was growing away from her and her God.

During the summer before his sophomore year, John ventured, for the first time, to the public library, a place his mother had strictly forbidden him to enter. "Too many dangerous ideas and false prophets," she would say. John stood awkwardly, working up the courage to approach the librarian.

"Do you have any books on snakes?" he managed to stammer when she looked at him.

"Is this for a school project?" she asked in return.

"No, ma'am. I just like snakes," John replied as if confessing a sin.

"What grade are you in?"

"I'll be starting tenth grade in the fall, ma'am."

"Well, this is a book for younger children," she said, walking briskly toward one of the bookshelves, "but it's very popular." She handed him a book called *Everything You Need to Know About Snakes and Other Scaly Reptiles*. A picture of a big, green snake graced the cover.

"I think that book has been here longer than I have," she said with a smile .

John took the book, running his hand over the worn cover. The spine had been taped several times to keep the book from falling apart.

"Can I read it?" he asked.

The librarian looked at him more closely. "Of course," she replied. "Do you have a library card?"

"No, ma'am," John replied. "Are they expensive?"

"No," she said, smiling again. "They're free. Once you have a library card, you can take the books home with you, if you bring them back on time."

John found a small chair in the corner and sat down, carefully opening the book. Inside were pictures of all kinds of snakes that he had never seen before—cobras, black mambas, and even ones that lived in the desert. There were descriptions of how each snake's venom worked, some capable of killing a person within minutes. He also saw pictures of snake charmers who played music to make the snakes dance.

When it was time for the library to close, the librarian tapped him on the shoulder.

"I see you're enjoying the book," she said.

"Yes, ma'am."

"Well, you can come back tomorrow if you like. Be sure to bring a piece of mail with your parent's name and address on it and I'll make you a library card."

"All right," John said and ran home. He pocketed a letter he didn't think his mother would miss and came back the next day. The librarian,

Mrs. Abernathy, took a shine to him and started setting aside books that she thought might interest him. He took the long walk to the library every day after school, and on Saturdays, he would tell his mother he was going to the woods to look for snakes.

The sun dropped quickly, the service ending. The final shovel of brown earth was placed gently on top of his mother's grave. John stood numbly, knowing that once he turned away, he would never return.

"She's in a better place," a husky voice said behind him. John turned to see the Reverend Elder reaching out a hand to him.

"Thank you, sir," John said, taking the hand and lowering his eyes.

"Your mother was a pillar of our community and will be sorely missed."

"Yes, sir," John replied, playing the dutiful son one more time. He greeted everyone, said all the right things, and effusively praised his mother's life and faith.

At last, Mrs. Abernathy approached him.

"How are you enjoying MIT, John?" she asked with a big smile.

John wrapped his arms around her and smiled brightly. "I didn't realize you would be here," he said. "There's so much I want to tell you."

Mrs. Abernathy had been John's savior and the only reason he had been accepted into MIT. She recognized the scope of his intelligence and curiosity and guided his education outside of the classroom, challenging him with more complex texts and concepts in history, literature, and science. His school grades went from a C average to straight A's.

By the time John was a junior, his personal studies had exceeded the high school's curriculum, especially in biology. Since biology was not a subject in which Mrs. Abernathy had much expertise, she steered him toward a professor at the local community college. During the fall of his senior year, she encouraged him to apply to the best universities, wrote glowing letters of recommendation, and supported him through every step of the application process. When he received a full scholarship from MIT, she could not have been more excited if John was her own son.

As the last of the congregants drifted away, John stood, rooted to the ground. A light rain fell, rivulets pooling in the freshly dug brown earth. John remembered the last conversation he had with his mother before he left for college.

"Blasphemer!" she screamed, slapping him on the sides of his head. "Heathen!"

"No, mama," he cried, his ears ringing under her blows.

"Who put these ideas in your head?" she asked, gripping him by the shoulders.

"No one," John said, tears streamed down his face.

"Liar," she replied. "I've a mind to go down to the library right now."

"No, mama, please," he pleaded. John was at least a foot taller than his mother, but he cringed in front of her.

"You deliberately disobeyed me. You threw open the door and invited Satan into our house. Well, I won't have it. I won't have the Devil in my house. You walk out that door and you just keep on walking, you hear me."

"Please, mama," was all he could reply. It was futile to explain he was no longer the same person she raised, how he yearned for knowledge, and how science was now his faith. He still loved her, still believed in God. Science was a way of understanding God, of understanding His creations.

"Get out of my sight," she said at last, turning away from him.

• • • •

AS HE STOOD ON THE banks of the Charles River, John watched the carved wooden boats of the crew team slice through the water. Behind him was Killian Court and the dome of the Maclaurin building, known to the students as building ten. In front of him, the Harvard bridge connected Cambridge to Boston. It was a beautiful, crisp, fall day and the sun was shining on the MIT campus, but it was not enough to raise his spirits. Since arriving, John had been struggling to fit in, feeling intimidated, overwhelmed, and lonely.

The other students seemed so much smarter and more accomplished than him, having attended some of the best high schools in the world. He was too shy and awkward to make friends, afraid to speak up in class, to risk exposing himself as a fraud. He came close to giving up, but there was nothing left for him at home. What would he say to Mrs. Abernathy after she had worked so hard to give him this opportunity?

The campus grew colder as fall turned to winter, and students spent most of their time inside their dorms or the libraries studying for midterms. John felt the pressure intensely. Choosing to leave was one thing, failing out another. The night before his first exam in organic chemistry, he heard a loud voice that shocked him out of his concentration. He turned, thinking someone was playing a prank on him, but there was no one there. John dreamed of his mother that night. She appeared to him as she was the day he had left, her graying hair pulled back, her eyes cold and severe.

"Blasphemer," she said. "You invited Satan into our house."

John woke in a cold sweat. *Blasphemer* echoing in his head.

John earned the highest grade in his class on his organic chemistry midterm. He also performed exceptionally well in his other classes, and for the first time, he started to believe that he could succeed at MIT.

The next semester, John took the class that would change his life, "Introduction to Xenobiology," taught by Dr. Samuel Friedmann. Dr. Friedmann was a prodigy, completing his doctorate at the age of twenty-three. In his lectures, he speculated on the possibility of an extraterrestrial origin for life on Earth. Dr. Friedmann radiated brilliance but also an intense, almost childish, curiosity. He jumped rapidly from topic to topic. In a single lecture he might cover diverse topics in geology and evolution, diving into the chemical structures of amino acids and end by discussing specific human genome variations. Many students found the lectures too eclectic and difficult to follow, but John was mesmerized.

At this time, John started to have a recurrent dream about his father. They were together on Mars, riding in a rover across the red rocks. Dark clouds rolled overhead. Streaks of lightning illuminated the landscape. His father was driving too fast, but he was not afraid.

"Are you having fun, John." His father turned to ask him.

"Yes, papa."

The rover bumped roughly over the rocks. When John looked down, he saw the ground covered with snakes. There were too many to avoid. The rover crushed them under its enormous wheels, tossing their mangled bodies into the air behind them. His father didn't seem to notice or slow down. He kept going faster and faster up a steep hill.

When they reached the top, his father stopped the rover and got out.

"Come on, John," he said, "I want to show you my world. Don't be afraid."

John looked at the ground, but the snakes were gone. He got out of the rover and stood next to his father on the top of a large cliff. Lightning struck the ground next to them. Suddenly, John began to fall. He reached out and grabbed onto a rock. His father stood above him, reaching down.

"Stop fooling around," his father said, annoyed.

"I'm not!" John yelled as the lightning struck again nearby.

"Take my hand," his father said, reaching down to him.

John stretched but he couldn't reach his father's hand.

"Come on, John," his father said. "Sometimes you remind me of your mother. You're stubborn, just like her."

"I'm not."

"You're not trying," his father said, getting angry. "Take my hand."

"I can't!" John screamed. "I can't hold on much longer. Help me, papa. Help me." John lost his grip on the rock and started to fall. That was when he always woke up.

As John started his sophomore year, he started to hear voices more frequently. Often, it was his mother's voice, but there were times that he could not identify who was speaking. The voice did not seem to belong to anybody that he knew or had known in the past. Regardless of who was speaking, however, none of the voices were like the soft, reassuring voice of Jesus he had heard when he was a child. The new voices were harsh and accusatory, berating him for his lack of faith.

This combined with the increased pressure of his schoolwork and lack of social support resulted in John falling into a severe depression. He was forced to take a leave of absence from his studies but was able to remain on campus to see the school psychiatrist. For the first time, John opened up to someone about his childhood, his conflicting emotions about his mother, and the father he had never known. After nine months of therapy and various treatments, he was able to return to classes.

John eventually graduated *summa cum laude*. He chose to remain at MIT to pursue both a master's and doctorate. Dr. Friedmann became his adviser and, when John finished his dissertation, offered him a post-doctoral fellowship. Dr. Friedmann's reputation had grown internationally and was rumored to be on the short list to become a director at the International Marine Exploration Agency (IMEA).

The two years John spent working directly with Dr. Friedmann were the happiest of his life, both personally and professionally. His fellowship ended, however, when Dr. Friedmann accepted his long-anticipated appointment as the director of the IMEA. Dr. Friedmann invited John to join him at the agency, but John decided to remain in academia, a world in which he had grown comfortable, accepting a tenured-track position at Caltech in Pasadena. With several months before the start of his teaching responsibilities, John decided to spend some time in San Francisco, a city he had fallen in love with while attending conferences over the years.

John hoped that having almost four months with nothing to do in a city he loved would improve his mental health, but he still found himself struggling with depression. He found a new, highly regarded psychiatrist, Dr. Siqueland. She adjusted his prescriptions, and after several months, he was feeling much better. Both the frequency and intensity of the voices had decreased to the point that he was able to ignore them most of the time. With a few weeks to go until he began working at Caltech, John was feeling optimistic about the future when he received a phone call from Dr. Friedmann.

• • • •

"TEN THOUSAND FIVE HUNDRED meters," the pilot said as the bathyscaphe descended. "We are now deeper than any human being has ever traveled."

Dr. Friedmann felt a glow of anticipation as he approached the culmination of years of challenging work and a significant professional gamble.

"Iridium concentration is .00167 parts per million," his colleague Dr. Liu said, reading a bank of monitors. "Starting real-time genome sequencing."

Dr. Friedmann peered out the large window above his console, the alien underwater landscape lit by bright spotlights mounted on the top of the vehicle. A goblin shark drifted past, its distinctive snout gliding down at an angle, distorting when it passed the edges of the thick plastic window.

"I can confirm the presence of alternate nucleic acids: CeNA, XyNA, hDNA," Dr. Liu said.

The bathyscaphe was now heading almost straight down. Dr. Friedmann could see pillow lavas on the ocean floor, beautiful protruding shapes of basalt cooled by the near freezing ocean temperatures. The pilot leveled the vehicle, and they proceeded along the base of the canyon.

"There's a smoker ahead," the pilot said.

As they continued through the murky depths, a plume of what appeared to be thick, black smoke rose from a hydrothermal vent.

"Fluid temperatures at the vent are approximately three hundred and seventy degrees," Dr. Liu said. " I can detect the presence of chemosynthetic bacteria."

They passed over the vent, gliding silently over the deep ocean floor.

"Eleven thousand meters," said the pilot. "External pressure is over one thousand bar."

"There," said Dr. Friedmann, pointing at the navigation screen. "I think I see an opening in the canyon wall."

"Iridium concentration has increased to .00239 parts per million," Dr. Liu said. The bathyscaphe glided toward a wide cavern cut into the wall of the canyon.

"Full stop," said Dr. Friedmann. They hung motionless. The lights of the bathyscaphe revealed nothing but darkness.

"What could have created a cavern like this?" Dr. Friedmann asked.

"It's impossible to say without further study," Dr. Liu replied.

The pilot pointed to the navigation screen. "The cavern extends back for at least ninety meters."

"Let's proceed cautiously," Dr. Friedmann said.

"Contact with the surface has been lost," Dr. Liu whispered. The only sound was the hum of the motors. Dr. Friedmann peered into the dimly illuminated space in front of the vessel. The cavern walls widened, then sloped down.

"Approaching twelve thousand meters," the pilot said.

The bathyscaphe continued to descend.

"We are now entering the core-mantle," Dr. Liu said. The vessel continued down for another ninety meters before leveling out. "The rock below us is an ancient ocean floor."

The vessel pushed through the inky blackness, the spotlights illuminating only ten meters in front of them.

"Iridium concentration has increased to .00591 parts per million," Dr. Liu said. "We are also picking up the presence of more alternate nucleic acids."

"There appears to be another cavern up ahead," the pilot said.

"I see it," Dr. Friedmann said, barely able to contain his excitement. The cavern walls angled upward. The crew became aware of a faint glow reflecting off the cavern walls in front of them. Dr. Friedmann thought it might be his persistence of vision after staring at an area illuminated by the powerful lights attached to the top of the bathyscape and then trying to peer into the darkness. To test this theory, he focused on a portion of the wall away from the spotlights, closed his eyes, waited sixty seconds, and opened them again. The glow was unmistakable.

"Could that be bioluminescence?" he asked Dr. Liu.

"We need to get closer," she replied.

The tunnel turned sharply to the right, the glow increasing. The bathyscape followed the curve of the wall and emerged into an enormous cavern. As the vessel angled upward, they stared in awe at an enormous object floating in the center of the chamber, swaying gently in the water's current. It appeared to have a large, rounded body with long, spindly tentacles dangling in all directions, like an enormous jellyfish. The surface of the object shimmered and emitted a subtly shifting range of color patterns. They stared, dumbfounded, unable to fathom the object that lay before them. Finally, Dr. Friedmann broke the silence. "My God," he said, "it's beautiful."

· · · ·

"HOW WOULD YOU LIKE to join me in exploring one of the most exciting discoveries in the history of this planet?" Dr. Friedmann asked when John picked up the phone.

"Dr. Friedmann?" he replied stupidly. There was no mistaking either the voice or the enthusiasm of his postdoctoral advisor.

"Honestly, this is the chance of a lifetime," Dr. Friedmann continued. "I know you are about to settle into your position at Caltech, and I can't go into any details until you've signed your life away, but trust me, it's worth it. Catch the next flight out here and let me know as soon as you arrive."

There was more to the call, but that was all John remembered as his plane started its descent. The International Marine Exploration Institute came into view, perched on a spit of land that jutted out into the Ligurian Sea. The building was designed to appear like the top half of a breaching humpback whale, its blue-gray tiles glistening in the sun. But the interior was even more beautiful. Once John passed through security, he looked up to see a wide, beautifully curved foyer, the walls adorned with ocean-colored lights. Underwater sounds played softly from speakers hidden throughout the hall.

Dr. Friedmann was waiting for John when he arrived in the conference room. "Glad you could make it," he said, taking John's hand warmly and rising. "You know Dr. Liu," he continued.

"Yes," John said, shaking Dr. Liu's hand. Dr. Ann Liu was one of the preeminent abiogenesis researchers in the world. During the early part of her career, she had studied the origin of peptides in hydrothermal vents. After years of work, and over fifty publications, she became skeptical that any known chemical reactions could be sufficient to explain the origins of organic life on Earth. Startling her colleagues, she quit her tenured teaching position at the California Institute of Technology and began working with Dr. Friedmann.

Dr. Friedmann, John's former mentor and postdoctoral supervisor, had devoted his research to investigating the possibility that life on Earth had originated in space. Following his appointment as Director of Xenobiology in 2065, Dr. Friedmann invited Dr. Liu to join him at the International Marine Exploration Institute.

Physically and temperamentally, Dr. Liu was the opposite of Dr. Friedmann. She was five foot two inches tall, with a calm, introverted personality. Her long black hair, now graying, was pulled back with a single hair tie. Dr. Friedmann, on the other hand, was tall and typically wore tailored suits outside of the lab. He was an outstanding researcher but also thrived in the sharp-elbowed politics of the academic and intergovernmental agencies that funded his research.

Dr. Liu smiled warmly at John as he took a seat next to her. A large screen covering the far wall projected what appeared to be a grainy, underwater video feed. John could make out construction equipment and the outline of what appeared to be an underwater laboratory. An enormous object took up most of the screen. It was unlike anything John had ever seen. John stood, transfixed. He had seen plenty of strange underwater creatures, but none so large and beautiful.

There was something incongruous about the object. It had the appearance of an organic particle under extreme magnification and appeared to flicker. At first, John thought the flickering was caused by the video, but as he stared more closely, he realized that only the object itself was shimmering, not the surrounding equipment or rock formations. Dr. Friedmann cleared his throat, pulling John out of his trance.

"Meet HB-FLS-1," Dr. Friedmann said.

"What is it?" John asked.

"That is why we are here," Dr. Friedmann responded. "You read our paper on the unusual saturation of alternate nucleic acids near the Mariana Trench?"

"Of course," John replied.

"We discovered HB-FLS-1 on a subsequent visit to that site," Dr. Friedmann continued.

"I remember in your paper that you specified the presence of an unusually high concentration of iridium at the site," John said.

"Precisely, which would indicate the presence of an extraterrestrial object since iridium is such a rare element on Earth," Dr. Friedmann said, pleased John had read his paper carefully. "We discovered a correlation between the concentration of iridium with the presence of alternate nucleic acids at the site. This invisible trail led us deep into a trench and the object you see on the screen, HB-FLS-1."

"Why does it appear to be shimmering?" John asked, still mesmerized.

"Ahh," Dr. Friedmann replied. "That is the most interesting question, but unfortunately, I am not versed enough in the mathematics of quantum mechanics to even attempt an answer."

"Quantum?" John said incredulously. "Are you serious?"

"Quite," Dr. Friedmann replied, expressionless.

"That doesn't make any sense," John continued.

"No," replied Dr. Friedmann with the old twinkle in his eye. "Isn't it marvelous?" John stared at him for a moment and then back at the screen. "I have reached out to Dr. Magnus Snorrason at Reykjavík University, one of the top researchers in the field," Dr. Friedmann continued, "and I believe I have convinced him to join the project."

"So why am I here?" John asked.

"Because you are also one of the top researchers in your field," Dr. Friedmann replied. "I should know. I trained you."

• • • •

HB-FLS-1 WAS FOUND in the Mariana Trench at a depth of approximately twelve thousand meters. Construction of an underwater laboratory at such an extreme depth was an engineering challenge that required collaboration between the International Marine Exploration Agency (IMEA) and the International Space Exploration Agency (ISEA). Established in 2056, the twin agencies included twenty member nations who financed and collaborated on multiple research projects to improve living conditions on Earth and to explore off-world habitats.

The ISEA was responsible for constructing the first permanent colony on Mars. The experience gained in transporting construction materials and building a habitable environment on another planet made the ISEA the only organization capable of building the undersea research center. Working through the twin agencies ensured that all member countries had a stake in the research, heading off any political and territorial battles over the object known as HB-FLS-1.

The primary engineering challenge was the Artificial Pressure System, or APS, essential for life at the extreme depths of the lab. The APS used advanced shield technologies developed for the Mars colonies to create an artificial environment of lower pressure. The amount of energy needed to maintain the artificial pressure was immense. Two power sources in geographically distinct regions fed two dedicated underwater cables. An on-site battery storage facility, capable of maintaining pressure for up to ten minutes, provided a final failsafe to allow for an emergency evacuation if both power systems failed.

When the discovery of HB-FLS-1 was made public, scientists, politicians, and religious leaders from around the world weighed in with theories explaining its origin and purpose. Many saw the object as evidence of an all-powerful creator, while others contended that the discovery proved that intelligent life must have visited the planet at some point in the distant past. Speculation on the nature of the object ran rampant on the Internet and conspiracy theories quickly bubbled to the surface. The name HB-FLS-1 was too technical for the public imagination and the object was renamed "The Hand of God."

In response, the ISEA set up restrictive protocols for accessing the site, limited to personnel of the ISEA, IMEA, and a regulated number of intergovernmental agencies and private contractors. Dr. Friedmann and the International Marine Exploration Institute were placed in charge of managing the scientific research, while the ISEA was responsible for engineering and security. The lab was completed in September 2075. John was among the first group of scientists to relocate to the HB-FLS-1 Research Facility.

John flew to Guam and boarded the submarine, which would carry him to the site deep in the Mariana Trench. He had never descended to such an extreme depth. As the lab came into view, he marveled at the miraculous feat of engineering, allowing him to live and work so close to the Earth's mantle. And then HB-FLS-1 came into view. From a small window on the submarine, he could see the bottom half of the object and some of the tentacles floating in the water.

The submarine docked and John was met by the lab administrator, Dr. Efren Gabrillo. "Good afternoon, Dr. Haggerty," he said, extending his hand. "Dr. Friedmann asked me to show you around the facility."

"Thanks," John replied, ducking his head as he came through the airlock.

Dr. Gabrillo, formerly the director of the IMEA facility at Subic Bay in the Philippines, was of medium build with dark hair and round glasses. "There are two main sections," he said. "We are currently in Section A, which includes docking, storage and the 'Hab' modules. Let me show you to your quarters. I hope you're not claustrophobic." He laughed.

They walked down a narrow corridor with two rows of small, half-sized doors on both the top and bottom of each wall. Dr. Gabrillo stopped and tapped a keycard on the wall and one of the doors popped open. "Here we go," he said with a smile, "room 37A." He pressed a button on the keypad and the bed slid out. John hopped up and pressed another button. The bed slid back, and the lights turned on. He was in a space roughly seven feet by three feet with another three feet of headroom. John renamed his room, "the coffin." He hit his head every time he woke up for the first two weeks.

Dr. Gabrillo then led John to a small kitchen galley stocked with freeze-dried meals and a row of coffee machines. Next to the kitchen was a fitness center with a single treadmill and some free weights. As there was no day or night at the bottom of the ocean, the researchers worked around the clock. Everyone who wanted to use the gym was assigned a thirty-minute block every day. John was assigned a block that started at three in the morning.

The final stop of the tour of Section A was a room used for social gatherings known as the game room. Visitors could play cards, chess, or backgammon, and someone had even brought a ukelele from Hawaii. Alcohol was not permitted at the facility, but every Friday, there was a competition for who could create the best mocktail out of only ingredients found at the lab. Most were undrinkable fiascos, but a few found favor with the researchers and were mixed in larger quantities. John was partial to Love Potion #9i, which if you closed your eyes and plugged your nose, almost tasted like a dirty martini.

Section B was much larger and contained the labs and conference rooms. The researchers were separated into two teams. Dr. Liu led a team of twenty-five astrobiologists spread across eight research projects. The astrophysics team had eighteen researchers working on five projects under the supervision of Dr. Snorrason. Dr. Friedmann split his time between the teams and made all progress reports directly to the ISEA. In addition to the researchers, there was one member of the support crew and two full-time engineers.

Once a month, a supply ship would replenish the food stores, and for a few days after, everyone enjoyed the luxury of fresh fish, meat, and veggies mixed in with their freeze-dried meals. John grew accustomed to his new schedule; he woke at 2:45 a.m. each morning and changed into his workout clothes before going to the fitness center. After his workout, he'd grab a quick breakfast from the cafeteria and head off to the lab.

Every day at ten a.m., the astrobiology team would assemble in the conference room for a meeting conducted by Dr. Liu. After the meeting, John would work steadily, with breaks for lunch and dinner, until about eight p.m. Once a week on Fridays, Dr. Friedmann presided over a full staff meeting. Dr. Liu would report on behalf of the biogenetics team, often referencing John's work.

John considered himself to be an excellent chess player, but he met his match in Dr. Snorrason. Tall, thin, and blond, Dr. Magnus Snorrason had a quiet demeanor that belied his extraordinary intellect. He worked long hours, rarely making an appearance in the game room. When he did, he came to play chess.

"You play well," Magnus said after beating John for the third consecutive game.

"Thanks, I don't feel that way when I play you," John replied with a smile.

"You need to take more risks," he said gently. "You had an opportunity in the last game, but you chose to protect your rook."

"I regretted that move almost as soon as I made it," John said, leaning back in his chair. "Would you mind if I asked you some questions about HB-FLS-1?"

"Not at all," Dr. Snorrason replied.

"Why do you believe the object is part of a quantum system? I've thought quantum mechanics was only applicable to microscopic systems."

"It is only a working theory of course, but I believe it's the most logical interpretation of our observations." Dr. Snorrason said modestly, "We have demonstrated that the properties quantum mechanics hold for complex molecules with thousands of atoms. There is no reason, therefore, to believe that, under the right circumstances, these properties may not apply to an object of any size."

"I read your team's analysis of the shimmering effect. The object is visible for exactly one out of every three microseconds, although the exact microsecond did not follow any recognizable pattern."

"Precisely," Dr. Snorrason said, always happy to discuss his work. "HB-FLS-1 appears to exist in three different physical locations simultaneously. In other words, we may be looking at Schrödinger's cat."

"What about the Heisenberg uncertainty principle?"

"Since it is impossible to predict during which microsecond the object is present in any given physical location, the uncertainty principle is upheld."

"And since the object is so large, there is no observer effect."

"Correct," Dr. Snorrason replied.

"Where do you think the other two instances might be?"

"It is impossible to say but I think we can safely say they would be somewhere in the known Universe." John could not quite tell if this was a joke.

Dr. Liu assigned John the task of investigating the chemical processes by which HB-FLS-1 produced nucleic acids. HB-FLS-1 had long tentacles, like a jellyfish, which slowly changed in both size and shape. New tentacles would occasionally appear on the surface of the object while other tentacles contracted until they were reabsorbed into the main body. The nucleic acids emitted by the object seemed to be produced by the tentacles themselves. Each individual tentacle generated a single nucleic acid, but there appeared to be no correlation between the length or thickness of the tentacle and the chemical structure of the nucleic acid produced.

Still more incredible, some of these tentacles appeared to extend past the lithosphere-asthenosphere boundary, implying that the object was present during the early phases of Earth's formation. It was impossible to determine how long or how far these tentacles spread underneath the Earth's surface. It was as if HB-FLS-1 had extended deep roots into the planet.

John began his research by studying the molecular makeup of HB-FLS-1's tentacles. The movements of each tentacle were independent yet seemed to be coordinated with the others. There was no contact or overlap. But he could not identify any means of communication between the tentacles and the body. Since the main body of the object was part of a quantum system, only physically present one third of the time, and the tentacles were always present, there could not be any physical connection.

High-resolution imaging had revealed a one-nanometer gap between the tentacles and the main body of HB-FLS-1. Dr. Friedmann hypothesized that the tentacles were not part of HB-FLS-1 but were separate organisms with their own distinct chemical structures. This meant that each tentacle had a different nucleic acid composition and was in a Darwinian competition with the other tentacles to replicate its own body chemistry.

John's next step was to perform a physical analysis of each tentacle, but he discovered that the tentacles did not like to be touched. At first, he tried to snip a small piece off the end of a relatively short tentacle, but every time he got close, the tentacle would curl away from him. He then tried to scrape the surface of the tentacle near the base, hoping to get some cells for analysis, but despite its flexibility, the surface was remarkably resilient to even the sharpest instruments.

He had been feeling defeated until he made a remarkable discovery—seawater collected at the tip of each tentacle contained distinct molecular components. This discovery was his biggest breakthrough and gave him a newfound sense of pride in his work. More than just clarity, it gave him purpose. It was the first step in making a meaningful contribution to the project. Now he just had to analyze each of the many tentacles not buried in the Earth.

• • • •

AS JOHN'S WORKLOAD increased at the lab, he realized that while his new regimen of medications was more effective in silencing the voices, he was having more frequent headaches and difficulty concentrating for extended periods. For the first few months, he was so engaged and stimulated by his work, the side effects were not too disruptive.

He enjoyed spending time in the game room with the other researchers who were both extremely intelligent and a lot of fun. Typically shy, John found himself joining sing-alongs and participating in charades and other party games. But, as time passed, his headaches increased in frequency and intensity, causing him to become more irritable and making it difficult to work through many of the social gatherings.

He struggled to maintain his concentration. As the weeks passed, he became increasingly frustrated as his performance began to decline. He was desperate to find a way to improve his focus and keep up the pace of work expected of him, or that he expected of himself. John began upping the amount of coffee he drank during his working hours. The additional caffeine helped his concentration but aggravated his headaches and insomnia.

After several unproductive weeks, John tapered down on his medications. His regimen consisted of three prescriptions: eight pills taken throughout the day. The first medicine consisted of four capsules, two taken in the morning and two at night. John skipped one capsule at night, reducing his dosage by twenty-five percent. The second medication consisted of three pills taken one every eight hours. He was able to reduce this dosage by one-third, taking one pill every twelve hours. The third medication consisted of only one tablet per day. The tablets were small and crumbled easily. He tried various methods of splitting the tablets using lab equipment but eventually pulverized them and weighed out a new seventy-five percent dosage.

By the second week of his new regimen, he found his concentration had improved slightly. He was able to reduce his caffeine intake and had fewer headaches. Encouraged, he started to skip another capsule of the first medication, reducing his dosage to fifty percent, and weighed out a fifty-percent dose of the third medication, leaving the second medication at two-thirds of the prescribed amount. Once again, he noticed improvements over time. He was more productive, his mood increased, and the debilitating headaches were less frequent.

His inventory of the molecular composition of the seawater near the tip of all the accessible tentacles was nearly complete. He packaged the data and requested assistance from a data scientist on the surface to train a classification model based on the attributes of the molecular composition of the seawater near a given tentacle and the amino acid generated by that tentacle. Once the precision of this model was sufficient, they would calculate the Shapley Additive Explanations (SHAP) values to understand the contribution of each molecular attribute to the generated amino acid.

"Blasphemer!"

The voice shocked him out of his concentration.

"Heathen! Defiler of the Word of God!"

John closed his eyes. He lowered his head into his hands and massaged his temples. The voice echoed as if bouncing around the inside of his skull.

He walked slowly back to "the coffin" and lay down. He breathed deeply, holding each breath for several seconds, practicing the relaxation techniques he learned in college.

"You invited Satan into our house," the voice continued. John lay still, concentrating on his breathing. The incident passed and he continued working that day. But over the next few days, the voices became more frequent, causing him to flinch visibly by the sudden outbursts only he could hear. He thought about increasing his medications but did not want to risk having to reduce his workload again.

The next week, a new voice spoke to him. Unlike the others, this voice was calm and melodic. It almost sang to him, but the words of the song were unintelligible. When he became aware of its presence, singing softly on the edge of his subconscious, he stopped working and sat quietly, trying to isolate the song and decipher the words. He sat for a long time and his muscles relaxed, a feeling of serenity spread throughout his mind and body. He could not identify either the beginning or end of the melody. The voice was both musical and not musical, then, as abruptly as it had begun, it was gone. John sat at his desk, waiting, listening for its return, when a powerful sensation of exhaustion overwhelmed him. He returned to his quarters and fell into a deep sleep, awaking later to the sound of knocking.

"John? It's Dr. Friedmann. Are you alright?"

"Yes, hold on a minute," John said, trying to get his bearings. He sat up and smacked his head against the ceiling and it all came back to him. He opened the door, blinking.

"Are you feeling sick?" Dr. Friedmann asked.

"No, just exhausted," John replied with a weak smile.

"Perfectly understandable," Dr. Friedmann replied. "I think everyone is getting a little stir-crazy down here. How about a cup of coffee?"

"Sure, what time is it?" John asked.

"About eleven thirty a.m. on the surface. You missed the team meeting today, so I wanted to make sure everything was okay."

"The team meeting?" John said. "Isn't that on Friday?"

"Yes," said Dr. Friedmann hesitantly. "What day did you think it was?"

Realizing he had slept for more than twenty-four hours, John stumbled to his feet. "Sorry," he said, "I'm just a little groggy from sleep." He followed Dr. Friedmann to the galley.

"Dr. Liu speaks highly of your work," Dr. Friedmann said, leaning back in his chair.

"Thanks, but I don't feel like I've been making enough progress," John replied.

"I feel like that every day," Dr. Friedmann said with a smile. "I just want to make sure you're pacing yourself. This is a long-term project. I would rather have you take time as needed than get completely burned out. We've missed you at the social gatherings. It's important to take some time every day to relax and spend time with other people. Believe me, I know how easy it is to become too focused on your work, and if you need some real time off, there's room for two return passengers every month on the supply ship."

"I appreciate it, but I'm doing OK," John said, not meeting his old professor's eyes.

"I'm not trying to get rid of you," Dr. Friedmann said smiling, "quite the opposite." He leaned forward, clasping his hands in front of him. "I hope that after all these years you view me as a friend."

"I do."

"Then, as your friend, I want you to know you can come to me, at any time, if you need anything or just want someone to talk to about something other than HB-FLS-1."

"Thanks."

"So, how's the data prep coming?"

"Good. I should have it done by the end of next week," John said, relieved at the change of subject.

"Wonderful," Dr. Friedmann said, draining his coffee. "Then I will see you tomorrow." John sat for a few minutes and realized he was starving. He walked back to the cafeteria to rehydrate an omelet.

"Liar." His mother's voice chided him as he ate.

For the next few months, John was able to work effectively, while keeping the voices at bay. He increased the dosages of his prescriptions until he maximized his concentration during waking hours while keeping the side effects in check. Three separate data science teams worked on John's data analysis, but they yielded no statistically significant correlations. After almost nine months underwater, he was no closer to unraveling the mysteries HB-FLS-1 than when he arrived.

The melodic voice sang to him continually, like a faint song on the edge of his consciousness only occasionally coming into focus. When he was close to HB-FLS-1 in the water, the singing got louder and clearer. However, Dr. Friedmann and Dr. Snorrason confirmed that no sound waves could be detected from the object. It was as if John was the only person able to hear the melody. He wondered if the music was connected to the signals being transmitted from the object to its tentacles, which could not otherwise be detected.

His psychologists had never been able to provide a clear explanation for John's auditory hallucinations. As a child, he genuinely believed that Jesus spoke to him. When he was older and learned the details of his father's life and death on Mars, he believed the voices told him things that were true, that no one could have known at the time. But he was not sure. It was possible his subconscious had combined facts he learned about his father with his childhood memories. He learned about the malleability of memory formation in neurology, a subject which fascinated him almost as much as biology and evolution.

One day, John woke and became aware of the absence of the melodic voice. He did not remember when it stopped, but realizing it was gone, he felt a great emptiness. Only then did he appreciate how much that voice had calmed him, soothed him, and allowed him to work.

"Blasphemer," his mother's voice said in a barely audible whisper.

John rolled out of bed, took his medication, and walked to the galley for breakfast. Assuming the melodic voice was real and not an auditory hallucination, and was originating from HB-FLS-1, why was he the only person able to hear it? Why couldn't any of the sensitive instruments in the lab detect it? And why had the object suddenly stopped communicating? When he concentrated on the melody, he had the maddening sense that there was a meaning embedded in the song, but he could not decipher it, like a word on the tip of his tongue.

John walked to his lab and sat in front of his computer. He was missing something and decided to review every report generated by his colleagues on all aspects of HB-FLS-1, looking for any theory or observation that might provide a new perspective. His headaches returned and the voices plagued him throughout his waking hours, but he managed to push through the discomfort and sudden shocking orations. His sleep schedule became more erratic, and he stopped going to the gym or participating in any of the social gatherings, saving all his energy for his work.

John spent more time in the water, swimming around the object in his dive suit, the tentacles curling out of the way at his approach. Sometimes, he would speak to the object silently, reaching out with his mind, trying to hear the melody once more. He dreamed he reached out, touched it with his bare fingers, and was transformed. He felt a deep calm, a peace he could only imagine. His father came to him and wrapped his arms around him. John felt safe and warm when a bitter voice erupted in his mind.

"You invited Satan into our house!"

His mother's voice jolted him out of his dream. A blistering headache pounded in his temples, and he was in tears. He was unable to get out of bed that day, or the next.

Dr. Friedmann visited him again and forced him to sit and play with the other researchers. He struggled to make small talk and look like he was having fun.

The next day after the morning meeting, John stood, took one step, and collapsed. Dr. Friedmann ordered an emergency medical shuttle. Two days later, John was back on the surface.

• • • •

"WHEN DID YOU STOP TAKING your medications?" Dr. Siqueland asked. She was a tall and slender woman in her fifties with ginger hair and an aquiline nose, sitting with a small notebook in one hand and a pencil resting thoughtfully in the other.

"I started to taper down on my prescriptions about eight months ago. They were interfering with my ability to work," John replied. He sat in a comfortable chair facing Dr. Siqueland, a haggard look on his face. The room was bright, sunlight streaming through a large picture window on the opposite wall.

"You thought it was wise to adjust your own prescriptions?" she asked, barely managing to restrain her disapproval. "How much did you taper?"

"Between thirty and fifty percent."

"And when did the voices return?"

"A few weeks after I adjusted the prescription."

"And yet you continued with the lower dose?"

"I needed to work," John replied flatly.

"I honestly don't know what to say, John. I frankly didn't expect to see you again." She consulted her notebook. "We met three times almost a year ago, and then you simply disappeared."

"Yes," John replied weakly.

"Can you tell me why?"

"After our last meeting, I was offered an extraordinary opportunity to join a remote research project."

"What is the nature of the project?" Dr. Siqueland asked. She flipped her notebook backwards. "You told me when we first met that you worked for the International Marine Exploration Institute."

"Yes. I'm a xenobiologist."

"I'm afraid my Latin isn't that good. What's a xenobiologist?"

"Xeno comes from the Greek word Xenos, which means strange or foreign, or in our case, alien. I'm an alien biologist, or a biologist that studies life forms that did not originate on Earth."

"I would think you would work with the Space Institute rather than Marine Institute. Are there alien life forms in the ocean?"

"That's what we are trying to figure out. The project is classified and extremely remote. Security is high and communications with the surface are restricted."

"Which is why you never contacted my office?"

"Yes," John replied. "Before I left, I had one of the psychiatrists at the institute fill my prescriptions for a year.

"Being isolated for extended periods of time is difficult for anyone," Dr. Siqueland continued. "What side effects, specifically, were you experiencing that prevented you from working?"

"Lack of concentration, brain fog, and headaches," John replied. "I could power through the brain fog with caffeine, but I started to drink so much caffeine that the headaches became unbearable. That's when I started to adjust my medications."

Dr. Siqueland paused to consider him. John had lost a lot of weight. His eyes were red, and he was distracted, nervously twitching his foot while he spoke to her.

"Are you hearing the voices now?" she asked gently.

"Yes," he replied weakly.

"Do you know who's speaking?"

"It's my mother's voice but it's not my mother."

"What is the voice saying?"

"That I should leave ... That you are a false prophet ..."

"Do you believe I'm a false prophet?"

"I don't know," he said after a moment, lifting his head. He looked at her, but his eyes were vacant. He seemed utterly detached. And then, the moment passed. His muscles relaxed, and when he looked back at her, it was as if nothing happened.

Dr. Siqueland regarded him. "I don't think I can continue treating you, John. Communications may have been restricted at the site, but there's no reason you couldn't have contacted me before your departure."

"No," John said.

"I also think you were very reckless adjusting your own medications," she continued. "Why didn't you reach out to the psychiatrist who refilled your prescriptions?"

"I was afraid they would take me off the project."

"I understand that your work is very important to you," Dr. Siqueland said in a measured tone. "However, you cannot neglect your health. I wish you the best of luck and I urge you to find the care you need before returning to work."

"Thank you, Dr. Siqueland," John said, rising. "I appreciate your honesty."

• • • •

IT FELT GOOD TO BE back in San Francisco after spending close to a year living at the underwater lab. John took a deep breath and felt the warmth of the sun on his skin as he left Dr. Siqueland's office and walked along Sansome Street. A light fog snaked through the buildings, and as he reached California Street, he saw a cable car rumbling toward him. He jumped on impulsively, hanging on with one hand and feeling the cool wind on his face as the car started to climb Nob Hill. Old St. Mary's Cathedral came into view with its marvelous brick façade and clock tower.

John hopped off the cable car at the top of the hill near Huntington Park and walked to the center, where he stopped in front of Fountain of the Turtles. He visited the original Fontana delle Tartarughe in Rome years ago. The sun was shining at the top of the hill, reflecting off the water in the fountain as it poured into four large conch shells surrounding the basin. He continued walking through the park until he stood, staring up at Grace Cathedral.

He felt an inexplicable force pulling him toward the church. He moved quickly up the steps, halting in front of a grand set of bronze doors. They were a replica of the Ghiberti doors from the Baptistery of Florence Cathedral, which Michelangelo had famously named the "Gates of Paradise." There were twenty-eight panels. Most of the panels depicted scenes from the life of St. John the Baptist. The eight panels at the bottom represented the virtues of faith, hope, compassion, modesty, courage, moderation, righteousness, and wisdom.

"Blasphemer!" His mother's voice echoed in his head.

"No," he replied sharply, turning around to see if he had spoken out loud, but no one paid him any attention. Realizing what he wanted to do, John walked to the welcome desk.

"Good afternoon," the older woman at the desk said. "Would you like to purchase a ticket?"

"I've come to pray," John replied. "But I'd like to make a donation."

"Thank you," she replied, indicating the location of the donation box.

John put a generous donation in the box and walked silently, head bowed, down the aisle. He lit a candle for his mother, saying the first prayer he uttered in years. He prayed that she had found peace at last. John then took a seat in the pews at the rear of the church. He sat for a long time, head bent, thinking about his mother and Colton.

John became aware of a young woman sitting several rows in front of him, her head bowed. She had short hair, shaved on one side. He could hear her muffled sobs and see her shoulders shudder intermittently. There was so much misery in the world, he thought, closing his eyes and withdrawing into the darkness of his own thoughts. The voices spoke softly to him. He thought of his mother on her death bed, gasping for her last breath. He had looked into her eyes, hoping to see a moment of release. He wanted her to be in Heaven. He wanted to see it in her eyes, a look of transformation or joy. But there was nothing, just a final gasp, an expression of pain frozen on her face.

"You are looking for proof of God," a voice said softly in his head. It was a soothing, masculine voice. "You must have faith."

John opened his eyes, but of course, there was no one there. He watched the woman weeping in front of him and felt the urge to comfort her. He stood and moved to her row.

"Forgive me," he said. "Are you alright?"

She looked up at him for a moment and then, embarrassed, turned away.

"I'm sorry," John said, backing off.

"No," she said softly. "Please."

John sat next to her for what seemed like a long while, drifting back into his own thoughts.

"You're very kind," she said, bringing him back to the present.

"Is there anything I can do to help you?"

"No."

"Do you want to talk?" John asked. "I'm a good listener."

"That would be nice."

"Come on," he said, leading her up the aisle into the sunshine of the late afternoon. The sun was just starting to set behind the cathedral.

"My name is Virginia, Virginia Rappe, but my friends call me Ginny," she said as they walked across the park.

"John Haggerty," he replied, stopping and reaching out his hand to her. Her hands were small and frail, her fingers thin. Her skin was alabaster, almost translucent.

"How about the Top of the Mark?" he asked. "My treat, come on. It's been years since I've been there."

They rode the elevator in silence, stepping out into the luxurious dining room overlooking the city.

"Are you hungry?" he asked.

"Yes, but ..." she said hesitantly.

"Don't worry. I've been working remotely for a long time with nothing to spend my money on," he said reassuringly. "Besides, I'm starving."

It was early on a Tuesday evening, and they got a table by the window, looking over North Beach and Coit Tower.

"Were you working in space?" Ginny asked.

"The other direction," John said with a smile. "Underwater."

"Are you a scientist?"

"Yes," he replied, picking up the menu.

Ginny looked nervously around the restaurant. "Are you sure this isn't going to be too expensive?"

"It's fine. Get anything you like. I'm going to have steak—a real steak! And a glass of California Cabernet."

Ginny looked at the menu tentatively. "Would you pick something for me? I've never been in a restaurant like this before."

"Sure, do you eat meat?"

"No."

"All right. Do you like mushrooms?" John replied, scanning the menu.

"Yes."

"You're in luck. Morels are in season. They're the best mushrooms you'll ever try. Do you drink alcohol?"

"No. I'm sorry."

"Why are you sorry?"

"I don't know," she replied, looking a little overwhelmed. "I'm just not very good at this sort of thing. I'm afraid you'll be wasting your money on me."

"Don't be ridiculous," John replied with a smile. "Do you live here, in San Francisco?"

"No," she replied softly.

"Where's home?"

"Nowhere at the moment," she said with her eyes lowered. "I left home a few weeks ago. I just arrived in the city this morning. I don't know anyone, and I didn't know where else to go, so I went to the cathedral. I thought if I prayed ... but I ... it's just ... I'm just ... so stupid. I don't know what I'm doing here. I should go." She rose abruptly.

"Wait," John said. "Don't go, please."

"I don't even know you," she said, holding back the sobs.

"I know, and it's none of my business, but you're here now, and like I said, I'm a good listener." John reached out his hand to her.

"I can't," she said. "I'm sorry."

"Wait," John said, rising. "If you need a place to stay, I'm at the Westin St. Francis, room 1219. I promise I only want to help you."

"You're very kind," she replied and turned, covering her face, running back to the elevators.

John finished his meal, thinking about Ginny. He thought about her riding down the elevator from the restaurant and walking back to his hotel. The fog had rolled in, and the air was damp and wet. He was still thinking about her as he entered the St. Francis Hotel and rode the elevator up to his room. She was so vulnerable. He couldn't imagine where she might spend the night. She had probably never been away from home before. John flipped on the television and sat on the bed with his back propped against several pillows, flipping channels mindlessly until he fell asleep.

A knock on the door woke him. The television was still on. He looked at the clock and wiped his mouth—almost one thirty in the morning. There was another gentle knock. He staggered out of bed and walked to the door.

"Who is it?" he asked.

"Ginny." He heard her barely audible reply. John opened the door with the safety lock in place and glanced out. She stood in the hallway, a frightened look on her face.

"Just a minute," he said, closing and reopening the door. "Come in."

She entered the room quickly. "I'm sorry," she said. "I didn't want to come but I didn't have anywhere else to go."

"It's alright," he replied. "I was worried about you."

She perched on the edge of a chair and looked up at him. "I shouldn't have come."

"I'm glad you did. There's a pullout you can sleep on," he said, grabbing the cushions off the couch. He lifted out the bed and pulled two extra pillows out of the closet. "The bathroom is there. I'll be in the next room so you can have privacy. We can talk in the morning." He walked back to his bedroom. "Good night."

"Good night," she replied. "Thank you."

He closed the door and lay in bed, turning off the TV. It felt good that she trusted him enough to come to his hotel room. He heard the sink in the bathroom, then he rolled over and fell back to sleep.

He was awakened again in the middle of the night by her touch. She had slid into bed next to him. He opened his mouth to speak, but she put her hand over his lips and climbed on top of him. Her body was soft and warm. It had been a long time since he had been with a woman. She made love to him passionately, and when they were finished, she kissed him longingly and settled next to him, nestling her back against his chest. He wrapped his arms around her carefully, almost afraid that he might crush her small frame, and fell into a deep sleep.

In the morning, she was gone. John panicked for a moment, scanning the room to make sure nothing was missing. There was a note on the coffee table. "I didn't want to wake you. Thank you for last night. I'll be back before lunch." He took a long shower and got dressed. He hadn't realized how much he had yearned for the touch of a woman. The sex was nice. What stayed with him in the morning was the feel of her in his arms, the warmth of her skin, the beating of her heart.

He wondered if she would really come back when there was a knock on the door. She held two cups of coffee and some pastries on a plate.

"I thought you might be hungry," she said brightly.

"Thanks," he said, taking one of the cups.

• • • •

JOHN SPENT THE NEXT three weeks with Ginny, taking long walks, exploring the city, sitting in cafes, and thumbing through used bookstores. She was curious about his work and life at the lab yet said little about herself. She was an only child from a strict Catholic family in Omaha. Something had happened between her and her father, which forced her to leave. He asked her about it on several occasions, but she avoided his questions and would start to cry if he persisted.

Most days they returned to the hotel, ordered room service, and made love while waiting for the food to arrive, exchanging mischievous glances when the waiter rolled the cart into the room. She was a patient and gentle lover, and for the first time in a long time, John forgot about the lab, HB-FLS-1, and all the things that needed to be done when he returned. He still heard the voices, but they were muffled, and for the most part, he was able to ignore them. He was happier than he had ever been. But it couldn't last. He was scheduled to return to the lab at the end of the month, something he couldn't bring himself to tell her.

Ginny was extremely perceptive, and as their days together wound down, she became aware of his growing anxiety.

"I want you to come somewhere with me tomorrow?" she said one evening when they returned to the hotel.

"Where?" he asked.

"It's a surprise," she replied with a smile.

"Alright, I like surprises, I think," he replied. "Is it a good surprise?"

"You'll see," she replied coquettishly.

The next morning, they walked to Market Street and took the Muni to Duboce Park. She held his hand as they walked up Scott Street toward Alamo Square. She led him through an upscale neighborhood to a large, beautifully restored, Victorian house.

"What's this?" he asked.

"The surprise."

"You bought a house?" he asked with a half-smile.

"You'll see." She walked to the front door and pressed the doorbell.

After a few minutes, a young woman in her early twenties opened the door.

"Hi, Astra," she said. "My mom's waiting for you."

Astra? John thought.

She led him past a staircase, through a set of carved wooden doors and into a large sunny room in the back. The room was furnished like a temple and in the center was a large glass sculpture of HB-FLS-1 and a kneeling pillow placed carefully in front of it. A woman wearing an ornate dress sat on a richly embroidered chair. She was in her late fifties or early sixties with close-cropped brown hair and a round face.

"Astra. May you rest in the palm of Our Lord," she said calmly.

"May we rest together," Astra replied, kneeling in front of the sculpture.

John was almost too stunned to speak but managed to stammer, "What's going on? Astra?"

"Welcome, John Haggerty," the woman said flatly.

John walked over to the sculpture of HB-FLS-1. It was remarkably detailed and accurate. He then turned to Ginny, who was still kneeling in front of the sculpture.

"Ginny?" he said weakly. She looked up at him mutely. "God, I've been such a fool," he said, turning to leave.

"Stop!" the woman said with remarkable power in her voice. "John Haggerty, you have been called by Our Lord."

"Our Lord?" John replied, turning. "You mean HB-FLS-1?"

"Do not blaspheme in this house of worship."

"House of worship?" John said, finding his voice and his anger. He turned back to Ginny. "You knew about my work! This—us—everything," he continued, "it was all a set-up, to bring me here!"

"We must be prepared to sacrifice everything for Our Lord," she replied, refusing to meet his eyes.

"Sacrifice! I'm sorry it was such a sacrifice!" John spat at her.

"Silence!" the woman said, rising.

"You're all crazy," John said, leaving.

"Our Lord commands you," the woman said, but John kept walking.

"Yeah, well your Lord can command me all he wants." John turned toward the door. "I don't have to listen."

"Wait," Ginny called after him. John hesitated and looked at her. His face was scarlet. Tears stained his cheeks.

"What? What do you want to say, Astra?" He laced her name with sarcasm.

"Please don't go," she said weakly, tears welling in her eyes.

"Oh, you're good," he said. "Those tears ... so real."

"You have heard Our Lord's song," the woman said.

"What?" John asked, turning his attention to the older woman.

"Our Lord sings to you."

"I don't know what you mean," John replied. The woman closed her eyes and began to sing. She had a beautiful voice. John recognized the melody, the melody which only he could hear, the melody which had comforted and sustained him during his long months at the lab. She sang it perfectly. John staggered. "How? How could you possibly ...?"

"Come, John Haggerty," she continued. "I realize that you have many questions, and I apologize for how you were brought here. What Astra did she did at the bidding of Our Lord. Do not be angry with her. You have been chosen by Our Lord as Her Disciple."

• • • •

JOHN TRAVELED TO THE Naval Air Station in Alameda and composed a brief, encrypted message for Dr. Friedmann.

I need to remain on the surface for another month due to personal and health-related matters. I apologize for the delay, but am confident that, once I resolve these issues, I will be ready to continue my work. Thank you again for the opportunity to be a part of this amazing project, and I look forward to seeing you soon. –John

He then checked out of the St. Francis Hotel and moved into the temple. His room was not much bigger than his quarters in the lab. There were twenty-seven followers of Our Lord living in the temple: thirteen women and, with John, fourteen men. They all shared a single room. Dividers had been roughly assembled so that each person had their own private sleeping area with a mattress. On opposite ends of the room were two gender-neutral bathrooms, each equipped with three showers.

A gong rang at five thirty in the morning every day. A breakfast of quinoa and vegetables was eaten in enforced silence. Breakfast was followed by morning chores, then two hours of solitary contemplation. The leader of the group, known to her followers as The Divine Fasha, appeared after lunch. She would bless them and enter a deep trance in which she communicated directly with Our Lord. During her trances, she would sing in an unintelligible language. The song was the same as the one John heard at the lab, and it still had the power to calm and soothe him. Prayers were followed by more solitary contemplation, dinner, evening chores, and bedtime.

The Divine Fasha lived upstairs with her daughter, Sarre. There was also a spacious bedroom kept upstairs for Manthe Ellis. Mr. Ellis was a serial entrepreneur whose net worth was estimated to be over one trillion U.S. dollars. His first enterprise, SolarCom, started in 2067, built the fastest and most reliable satellite network between the Earth and Mars. With the profits from SolarCom, Ellis started a new venture, GAIa, whose mission was to advance the practical applications of general artificial intelligence. Both SolarCom and GAIa were ISEA subcontractors and played a significant role in the development of the Mars colony and the HB-FLS-1 research lab.

Mr. Ellis was a global celebrity and provocateur who liked to claim that GAIa systems would eventually make human intelligence insignificant. John saw him in the news often and followed his social media accounts when he was a student. Mr. Ellis visited the temple infrequently but was deeply involved in their activities and joined their prayer sessions virtually.

John managed to catch glimpses of Astra throughout the day, but they could never be alone together. Followers were forbidden from speaking to one another outside of spiritual discussions or in the completion of chores, and only then in a group setting. John ached for Astra. Being near her but unable to touch her was painful. He hoped for a sign, a glance, the slightest touch, any indication that their affair had meant something other than the fulfillment of her duty. But she remained distant, refusing to acknowledge him.

One morning, however, she came to him after breakfast.

"I am to bring you to The Divine Fasha," she said.

"All right," he replied. She turned, but he reached out and touched her arm. "Ginny?" he asked. "Was that your name before?"

"We mustn't speak," she replied, turning to face him.

"Just tell me that. I want to know that at least one thing you told me wasn't a lie."

"Yes," she replied quietly. "My name was Ginny. It is now Astra. Please, we mustn't keep Her Holiness waiting." She turned and continued up the darkened stairway.

Astra led John to the altar room, stepped out quickly, and closed the door behind her. He must not keep Her Holiness waiting, but he was sure she intended to keep him waiting, John thought walking over to the sculpture of HB-FLS-1. It was a remarkable work of art, twelve feet in diameter, constructed from blown glass, with no visible seams or imperfections. The colors were vibrant and the surface shimmered. More remarkably, it appeared to be an extremely accurate reproduction. Having spent almost a year studying the object, John knew the relative dimensions. Every aspect of the sculpture appeared correct to him. There were eleven tentacles of varying lengths. Some hung in the air, others disappeared beneath the floor. Glancing closely, he noticed that they did not connect to the body. There was the smallest gap, exactly as there was on HB-FLS-1.

"It is a divinely inspired gift from Our Lord," the Divine Fasha said, having entered the room silently.

Turning, John saw her standing behind him. How long had she been there?

"It's beautiful," John replied.

"Please address me as Your Holiness," she said, correcting him mildly. "Our Lord has spoken," she continued closing her eyes in reverence. "In one week, you are to return to the infidels."

"They're scientists, not infidels, Your Holiness," John replied.

"Silence!" she said abruptly, anger flashing out of her eyes, which had so recently appeared beatific. "Have you learned nothing in your time here? They are fools who would keep Our Lord from us."

"I don't understand, Your Holiness," John said. "Our Lord cannot be moved."

"Do not repeat their lies in my presence," she said. "Our Lord wishes to be free."

"How can you know that?"

"She speaks to me, John Haggerty, as she has spoken to you."

"I've heard the singing, but I can't understand the words."

"Because your mind is closed. You closed your mind to God when you were a child."

"How can you know that?"

"Our Lord has revealed many things to me. I know that you hear voices. You would do well to heed them, John Haggerty."

"No, that's not ..."

"Blasphemer!" she said in the same tone as the voice he heard so many times in his head.

"Stop it!"

"You hear the voice of your mother," she continued. "You dream of your father. Do you deny these things?"

"No."

"You are Her chosen disciple, but you turn your back on Her. You serve the infidels."

"I serve science," John said futilely.

"You seek truth, John Haggerty, not knowledge. You have confused them. Our Lord offers you truth. She speaks to me now. Take my hands," she said, reaching out to him.

John reached out and grasped her hands. As soon as their fingers touched, the music started, softly, in his head.

"Open your mind, John Haggerty. Open your heart to Our Lord."

The next morning at breakfast, John's movements were sluggish, and his eyes were heavy-lidded. The spoon in his hand trembled slightly as he stirred his coffee, a clear sign of his disorientation. His usual alertness and energy were absent, replaced by a sense of lethargy and confusion. His neck was stiff and painful, and he didn't feel like eating. Her Holiness suggested that he spend the rest of the day in quiet contemplation. Two days later, John boarded a plane, starting the long journey back to the lab. He was uncomfortable during the flight. His neck was still sore, and he could not find a comfortable position.

• • • •

JOHN FELT A THRILL of excitement as he stepped through the airlock. Dr. Friedmann and Dr. Liu were there to greet him.

"John," Dr. Friedmann said, beaming. He wrapped his arms around the younger man. "It's good to have you back."

"How are you?" Dr. Liu asked.

"Good," John replied. "Much better."

"Excellent," Dr. Friedmann replied. "You have been missed."

They walked to the large conference room. Dr. Friedmann poured three cups of coffee and they sat together. Dr. Liu flicked on the monitor.

"Let's catch you up," Dr. Friedmann said, "and please don't tell me how much better the coffee is on the surface."

"Or the food," said Dr. Liu longingly.

They spent most of the day reviewing the latest work from each of the research teams. Dr. Liu had personally continued John's research on the analysis of the tentacles and the relationship of the structure of individual tentacles to their generated amino acid.

"We realized that the tentacles expand and contract at a constant rate," Dr. Liu said. "We were therefore able to determine the age of the tentacles that are currently expanding."

"And for those that are contracting?" John asked.

"It is impossible to determine without knowing the length at which a given tentacle stopped expanding," Dr. Liu replied.

"Nor," continued Dr. Friedmann, "if there is a period of time between the expansion and contraction phase."

"And there is no correlation with any other physical characteristics, such as diameter?" John asked.

"No. Not that we can determine," replied Dr. Liu. "However, this information allows us to add a time sequence to the generated amino acids for the expanding tentacles."

"We are hoping to discover if these variations are deterministic," Dr. Friedmann continued. "In other words, is the object randomly generating each subsequent amino acid or is there a pattern? The answer to this question would provide our strongest insight into the nature of the object."

"How so?" John asked.

"As you know, there is no true algorithmic randomness. All random generators are in fact pseudorandom. They generate statistically random outputs using a deterministic and repeatable process. If this object is generating truly random outputs, that would be compelling evidence to support the theory that the object is a naturally occurring phenomenon."

"Yes," John said, his mind racing.

"And if there is a pattern, that would be compelling evidence to support the theory that the object was placed here by some form of intelligence."

John sat back, absorbing what Dr. Friedmann said.

"Why is this object here?" Dr. Friedmann continued. "That is, of course, the most important question. What is its purpose, its final cause in Aristotelian terms? I thought that we would only be able to speculate on this question after elucidating its material, efficient and formal causes. However, now that we can establish a temporal sequence, we can speculate on the object's purpose. The first theory, based on a truly random sequence of amino acids, is that the object is naturally occurring and was captured by Earth's gravity four and a half billion years ago."

"Like a galactic spore," John said.

"Yes," Dr. Friedmann continued. "In this case, there would be no final purpose. The distribution of life in the Universe would be a result of the random distribution of these, and perhaps similar objects."

"And the second theory?" John asked, knowing the answer but wanting to hear someone else say it.

"The second theory, based on a pseudorandom sequence of amino acids, is that the object was placed here deliberately by some form of intelligence."

"What about the geological record? Does that support either theory?"

"I'm afraid not," said Dr. Friedmann. "If the object was placed here, it was done very carefully, without leaving any evidence that the site was disturbed."

"And what about the three-state quantum system? Why is this object connected to two other locations?"

"At this time, we simply have no way of knowing," Dr. Friedmann replied. "You've only been gone a few months."

"Yes, of course," John said, sitting back in his chair and trying to absorb the implications of everything Dr. Friedmann said.

"We're all glad you're back, John," Dr. Liu said. "Your research has become of vital importance to this project."

"Thank you," John said. "I can't wait to get started."

For the first month, John was so involved in his work that he hardly gave a thought to his time on the surface: Ginny, Her Holiness, or his life at the temple. They all seemed like distant memories. He had resumed the adjusted dosages of his prescriptions, refilled for another year while he was on the surface. The voices were quiet, and he was content to immerse himself in the mysteries of HB-FLS-1.

But after a while, the memories returned. He awoke in the mornings thinking of Ginny, feeling her touch, remembering their nights together in the hotel. How had she targeted him? He had only been in San Francisco for a few days when they had met at Grace Cathedral. They must have been tracking him for a long time, perhaps they had been tracking everyone who worked on the project, looking for an opening, someone they could lure. She had played her part perfectly, manipulated him effortlessly. They seemed to know everything about him, about his past.

None of this would be difficult for someone with Manthe Ellis's resources and connections. The only thing John could not explain was how Her Holiness had sung the melody, the melody which only he could hear. Could she really have some sort of mental connection to HB-FLS-1? He found that impossible to believe. But he could not explain his own connection to the object. Why had it singled him out? If the voice returned, he would bring it to the attention of Dr. Friedmann to be studied like any other phenomenon related to HB-FLS-1.

The most puzzling question was why—why had they worked so hard to bring him to the temple in the first place? What did they want from him? Her Holiness had not asked him any questions about the facility or about HB-FLS-1. She spoke only of "liberating Our Lord." But what did that mean? The object could not, physically, be moved. Surely Manthe Ellis, given that both of his companies worked on the construction of the facility, had access to more detailed technical information than John could provide.

Dr. Friedmann, along with senior scientific and military leaders at the ISEA, were aware of what they referred to as the Ellis cult. The Divine Fasha staged regular demonstrations and protests, most recently at Dr. Friedmann's appearance at the United Nations in Geneva. She traveled frequently, recruiting at major cities around the world. The cult had grown in popularity, attracting prominent celebrities to the cause. While they issued no direct threats against the site, their constant calls to "Liberate Our Lord from the Infidels" could not be ignored.

The ISEA responded to the possibilities of an attack from the Ellis cult, non-ISEA nation states, or other bad actors, by stationing two battleships in surveillance above the site and tightening security at the lab. The increased security measures were implemented exclusively by ISEA personnel with the intention of keeping the details confidential. The researchers knew that something was being done to increase safety yet were unaware of the details.

John's recent collapse had also raised red flags among the top brass at the ISEA. A burned-out researcher could compromise security or damage essential systems. In response, Dr. Friedmann introduced a policy of mandatory vacations for every staff member. Every month, one researcher from both the astrobiology and astrophysics teams would take a break and return to the surface. Knowing their schedule in advance allowed the researchers to hand off critical work to their colleagues and avoid unnecessary delays or disruptions. When the first researchers returned from vacation, John was tempted to ask them if they had been contacted by a member of the cult. But doing so would require him to confess his own experience.

He longed for the return of the melodic voice. After an initial period of excitement, his work became more difficult, the headaches returned, he had trouble sleeping, and he struggled to maintain his concentration during his working hours. On top of that, he was frequently startled out of his concentration by the auditory hallucinations. He had not made any progress in deciphering a pattern to the temporal sequence of amino acids. Feeling frustrated and dissatisfied, his mood darkened. He withdrew from his colleagues, growing more edgy and impatient as the days passed. He worked at all hours, neglecting his gym slot or anything that might help him to relieve the pressure.

More troubling was that he found himself doing things he could not remember wanting or needing to do. The feeling was hard to describe. It started with simple things, such as finding himself in a part of the lab without being able to remember why he was there. These incidents were easy to ignore as the result of too much work and too little sleep. But, one day, he found himself in his wet suit, swimming near the boundary of the artificial pressure system. He could not remember putting on the wet suit or going through the airlocks into the water.

When John awoke one morning, he noticed the date was two days later than he had assumed it to be. He reviewed his work log and messages from the previous day and saw that he had, in fact, put in a full day's work, but he could not remember any of it. There were messages he had written to colleagues, sent from his workstation, that he could not remember writing. He reviewed the transcription from the previous day's meeting and saw that he had made his daily update, but he could not remember attending the meeting. None of his colleagues mentioned anything to him about the previous day being unusual.

John remembered his neck pain after leaving the temple. He probed the back of his neck, methodically applying deep pressure until he found a lump with a slight resistance in the middle. He recalled reading about a joint experimental program between the military and GAIa in which a chip constructed from human tissue was embedded into soldiers at the base of the spine. Over time, the chip was able to integrate with the synapses of the human brain. Soldiers could then be effectively programmed and centrally controlled by military commanders, combining the creativity and experience of fighting men with the central control and rapid response of robotic soldiers. In addition, soldiers would not be able to remember their actions on the battlefield and had significantly lower risk of PTSD. The program was terminated when a whistle blower at GAIa raised ethical concerns, resulting in a large-scale investigation and numerous news articles about the technology.

John pulled up the news archive and read everything published about the program. Sleep studies measuring unconscious brain activity were required for at least two weeks before the chips were installed. My God, he thought, it all made sense. They had been monitoring his brain activity at the temple while he slept, installing the chip before he returned to the lab. But what had they programmed him to do?

Whatever it was, he could not escape the feeling that he now represented a very real risk to the lab, his colleagues, and HB-FLS-1.

John decided to take another leave of absence and have the chip removed by a private doctor on the surface. It would raise red flags since his recent return, but he was confident that Dr. Friedmann would understand and facilitate the trip. If he admitted the truth about his time at the temple or the embedded device, he had no doubt he would be permanently banned from the site.

He visited Dr. Friedmann in his office later that day to discuss taking leave.

"Are you sure everything's all right, John?" Dr. Friedmann asked, a note of real concern in his voice.

"Yes, I just ..." John stated, then paused. "You know about my medical history and that I'm on several medications to control the symptoms, particularly the auditory hallucinations."

"Yes," Dr. Friedmann replied thoughtfully.

"I've been having difficulty balancing the side effects of the medications with my workload. I've been suffering from headaches and a lack of concentration."

"You have been pushing yourself too hard, John," Dr. Friedmann said. "A project like this requires pacing yourself. You need time for rest, exercise, and social activities."

"I know," John replied genuinely. "I stopped seeing my psychiatrist, or rather she stopped seeing me, and I really need to find someone to help me adjust my prescriptions."

"As you know, there's only room on the monthly shuttle for two people," Dr. Friedmann said. "It would mean another emergency call."

"I know," John replied, "and I'm sorry."

"Don't be sorry," replied Dr. Friedmann. "I'm glad you came to me, and I want to get you the help you need. Would you be willing to remain in the station for at least another month? I'll arrange virtual meetings with another psychiatrist. Dr. Liu and I will reduce your workload in the short term. But I want you to promise me that you'll take care of yourself, meaning regular sleep, exercise, and participating in social activities. If, after another month, you still feel the need to return to the surface, that can be arranged."

"All right, I'll try," John replied, "and thanks." He returned to his office disheartened. How could he refuse such a generous offer?

"Blasphemer!" the voice shook him with its intensity.

He returned to his quarters and lay on the bed, rubbing his temples.

"Liar!" his mother's voice spat at him. "You invited Satan into our house."

John theorized that the implant in his brain was liberating his subconscious while he was awake, increasing his auditory hallucinations. The GAIa chip connected directly to his unconscious mind and bypassed his conscious control or even his conscious awareness of its influence.

John lay in bed, eyes closed, concentrating on his breathing. He wished he had learned to meditate properly. Every time he tried, he felt itchy and uncomfortable. He thought back to the time he had spent with Colton as a child, sitting and listening to the sounds of the forest. He remembered how Colton could calm him with a single touch from his large hand. He imagined Colton's hand on his shoulder and tried to remember the sounds of the forest.

"We must be prepared to sacrifice everything for Our Lord." Ginny's voice spoke softly in his ears.

He tried to recall if he had seen Ginny when he entered Grace Cathedral, or if she had slipped in after him. She must have followed him from Dr. Siqueland's office. He had been such an easy target.

John awoke twelve hours later with no memory of where he had been. Terrified of what he could have done, he rose and rushed to the medical supply room. He grabbed some numbing cream, a scalpel, a package of large gauze bandages, and a roll of medical tape. Using the gauze, he smeared the numbing cream along the back of his neck and sat, waiting for it to take effect. When he could not feel anything as he poked and prodded at the base of his neck, he picked up the scalpel, but as he tried to lift his arm, it would not move, as if it was paralyzed. He struggled against his own body. He shook, concentrating on trying to force his muscles to move. But it was no use. The scalpel fell uselessly to the ground. He was no longer in control of his mind.

"Blasphemer!"

John picked up the scalpel and put it back on the shelf.

"John Haggerty, you have been called by Our Lord." Her Holiness spoke to him.

John fell to his knees and blacked out. He awakened once more in his bed the next day. He had to know what he was doing, what they were making him do. John walked to his office and grabbed one of the small cameras used to record HB-FLS-1. It was compact, waterproof, and could record several days of video before running out of battery. They were so useful, the researchers often wore them around their arms so they wouldn't have to run back to the lab if they needed one on the spot.

John immediately cut off the thought. He forced his mind to think of something else. He had to hide the idea from his own subconscious. He looked around the office, his eyes settling on an unused power cord. Holding it by the end, he whipped it over his shoulder, like a flagellant. His back screamed in pain as the cord slapped his skin. Yes, he thought. The pain would focus his mind on the present. He whipped himself over and over. When he thought he was on the verge of passing out, he turned on the camera, wrapped it around his arm, and fainted.

He awoke from the dream of his father on Mars, the one he had been having since college. John lay in bed, rubbing his eyes. He reached for his arm and felt the video camera. He rose quickly and made his way to his office.

He pulled the camera off his arm, but when he tried to plug it into his workstation, his hand froze, quivered, and hung in the air. John picked up the power cable and whipped himself mercilessly on the back. He focused his mind on the pain. Straining, he managed to plug in the video camera and transferred the file to his private directory. He whipped himself whenever he felt the chip about to block his actions. He opened the file, dragging his finger to scan through the timeline until the camera moved out of his office.

"You invited Satan into our house!" his mother screamed at him.

The camera on his arm was pointed at an oblique angle and bounced as he moved. He watched as he made his way through a locked door into a restricted area.

"We must be prepared to sacrifice everything for Our Lord," Ginny said.

The battery backup. My God, he was doing something to the battery backup.

"Blasphemer!"

John whipped himself violently. He couldn't see what he was doing with his hands. The camera bounced again. It appeared as if he was climbing down a metal ladder. He could hear the hum of electricity.

Whip!

At the bottom of the ladder was a large room with electrical equipment and two enormous junction boxes. This must be where the power cables entered the facility.

Whip!

What was he doing with his hands? He stayed in the room for a long time, over thirty minutes, but all John could see was the wall and some electrical equipment.

Whip!

The pain was intense. Blood soaked the back of his shirt. He was on the move again in the video, back in his office, and now in the conference room. He heard his voice speaking, giving his daily report. Back to his office and then to his bunk. The video ended. John purged the file. He was planning to destroy the artificial pressure system, crushing everyone and everything instantly.

Whip!

He couldn't let that happen. He couldn't ...

"Blasphemer! You brought Satan into our house!" his mother screamed.

And then he heard the melody. Soft, barely perceptible, but it soothed his mind. She called to him, the song growing in intensity, the words unintelligible. John left his office and walked to the changing room. He pulled on his wet suit and stepped into the airlock. The next thing he knew, he was in the water, swimming toward HB-FLS-1.

· · · ·

I FEEL HER CALLING, singing to me as I swim toward her. The cuts on my back sting in the brine, but my mind is clear, the pain rooting me to the present. The voices subside. A sense of peaceful awareness settles over me. I feel and do not feel the cold. I see and do not see the blue-green shadows in the water. I hear and do not hear my breathing. I am both watching myself swim and swimming. I am both inside of, and outside of, time. Her voice, so pure, so beautiful it hurts my ears with longing.

She reaches for me as my father had reached for me. I hear my father say, "Take my hand, John."

I remove my diving glove and watch it float silently away.

"I'm coming, papa."

I reach and stretch, afraid that at any moment, I might fall.

· · · ·

JOHN HAGGERTY EXTENDED his bare hand, touching the tip of the tentacle that hung before him. When he made contact, his body shimmered for an instant and was gone, leaving his empty wet suit floating lifelessly in the water.

· · · ·

THE HAND OF GOD will continue in *The Ganymede Anomaly,* coming soon...

Don't miss out!

Visit the website below and you can sign up to receive emails whenever Darin S. Cape publishes a new book. There's no charge and no obligation.

https://books2read.com/r/B-A-BSRAB-EBPOC

BOOKS 2 READ

Connecting independent readers to independent writers.

About the Author

Darin S. Cape is the sound of one-hand clapping.
Read more at https://www.darin-s-cape.com/.

About the Publisher

SHP Comics is here to bring you innovative and thrilling stories that you won't find anywhere else! Explore our edgy, imaginative worlds that will thrill and scare you, and might just blow your mind! We're comics and stories on the edge.

Read more at https://www.shpcomics.com.

Milton Keynes UK
Ingram Content Group UK Ltd.
UKHW040625041123
431893UK00001B/123